FEARLESS
FISH

GOOF-OFF
GOOSE

HEALTHY
HIPPO

IMITATING
IGUANA

JEALOUS
JACKAL

POSITIVE
PIG

QUESTIONING
QUAIL

RESPONSIBLE
RABBIT

SMARTY
STORK

TEMPER TANTRUM
TURTLE

YAKETY
YAK

ZANY
ZEBRA

HERE THEY ARE

SWEET PICKLES ®

**All twenty-six of them
in stories with giggles
and tickles and awful pickles**

this
book
belongs
to

Christina Simpson

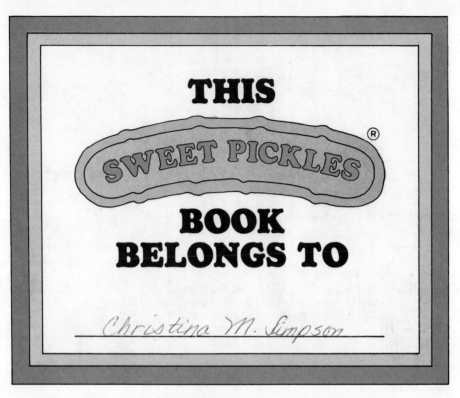

THIS
SWEET PICKLES ®
BOOK
BELONGS TO

Christina M. Simpson

In the world of *Sweet Pickles*, each animal gets into a pickle because of an all too human personality trait.
This book is about Fearless Fish, the town daredevil. She carooms around town on her motorcycle wearing her special SCOBA helmet (Self-Contained Out-of-water Breathing Apparatus) and tries to prove how fearless she is.

Other Books in the Sweet Pickles Series:

Library of Congress Cataloging in Publication Data

Reinach, Jacquelyn.
  Fish and flips.

  (Sweet Pickles series)
  SUMMARY: Fish is not afraid to try outrageous
motorcycle stunts, even though everyone warns her not to.
  [1. Fishes—Fiction] I. Hefter, Richard.
II. Title. III. Series.
PZ7.R2747Fh   [E]   77-14577
ISBN: 0-03-042016-4

Copyright © 1977 Euphrosyne, Incorporated

Printed in the United States of America

Weekly Reader Books' Edition

Weekly Reader Books presents

FISH
AND
FLIPS

Written by Jacquelyn Reinach
Illustrated by Richard Hefter

Edited by Ruth Lerner Perle

Holt, Rinehart and Winston · New York

VROOM!
Fish raced around town on her motorcycle delivering the morning newspapers.
VROOM!
She sped up and down Fourth Street, neatly slinging papers onto doorsteps.
VROOM!
She zoomed around to Fifth and increased speed. "Zowie!" she cried, checking her time. "Today is my best speed record yet. I am the greatest!"

VROOM!

Fish swerved into the apartment house driveway.

"Look out!" shouted Alligator. "You almost ran over my tail and it's your fault!"

"Don't blow a gasket!" laughed Fish. "I know what I'm doing. I am the greatest!"

"Nyaah!" screeched Nightingale. "Speed demon! Show-off!"

"Yes!" yelled Fish. "I *love* to show off what I can do!" She raced her motor and called loudly, "COME TO THE PARK AND WATCH ME SHOW OFF MY NEW MOTORCYCLE FLIP!"

"A motorcycle flip?" said Dog. "You shouldn't do that, Fish. It's dangerous."

"They do it all the time on TV," said Fish. "I'm not afraid!"

Everybody ran to the park to watch.

Fish jumped up on her motorcycle and bowed to the crowd. "I will now show you my fantastic new motorcycle flip," she announced. "I will go *up* the slide and flip through the air, all the way over to Fifth Street!"

"Oooooooh!" cried everybody.

"Don't do it! Please don't do it!" cried Walrus. "If you flip through the air, you could crash into a tree. Then you'd fall down and hurt yourself. And they'll have to call an ambulance and…"

"Don't worry, Walrus," smiled Fish. "I can do it. I'm not afraid."

Fish kicked into gear and zoomed across the park.

VROOM!
Up the slide, over the top and off into the air she went.

VROOM!
She flipped over the trees and out to Fifth Street.

VROOM!
She landed with a squeal of brakes!

Everybody came running out of the park, clapping and cheering.

"Wow!" cried Dog. "I didn't think you could do it but you did!"

"Amazing!" chuckled Zebra.

"Incredible!" smiled Lion.

"Big deal!" sneered Nightingale. "That was nothing!"

"You're right," said Fish. "I can do much better than that. Come back tomorrow. I'll fix up my special chopper and I'll jump over nine cars on Main Street."

"Oh, no!" cried Walrus. "You could *really* hurt yourself!"

"Don't worry, Walrus," said Fish. "I'm not afraid."

"I wish you were," said Walrus. "There's an awful lot to be afraid of!"

The next day everybody helped Fish get ready for her
nine car jump.
Fish adjusted her helmet, bowed to the crowd and
roared off.

VROOM!

Everyone shouted as Fish jumped over car after car. "ONE...TWO...THREE...FOUR...FIVE..."

Walrus put both hands over his eyes and then peeked a little.

"...SIX...SEVEN...EIGHT...NINE!"

"She did it!" screamed Stork. "A nine car motorcycle jump and a perfect landing!"

The crowd burst into wild cheers.

Fish grinned and said, "If you think *that* was good, come back tomorrow and I'll show you something even *better*! I'll gas up my jet-propelled Flycycle and do a giant leap all the way across the river!"

Everybody gasped. "A leap across the *river*?"

"No, no, no, no!" cried Walrus. "*Nobody* can leap across the river on a motorcycle!"

"*I* can!" said Fish.

"Aren't you afraid of *anything*?" moaned Walrus.

"Nope!" said Fish.

"Listen," said Camel. "It's one thing not to be afraid, and another to be foolish. I don't think you should do it."

"You don't understand," said Fish. "I am the greatest. Besides, my Flycycle is no ordinary motorcycle!"

"Goody!" snickered Nightingale. "Call the ambulance now!"

The next day, Fish got ready for her giant leap across the river.

Everyone gathered on the bridge to watch.

Fish was ready.

She jumped on the Flycycle, waved to the crowd and cried, "READY!"

"You'll be sorrrry!" giggled Nightingale.

"SET!"

"No!" wailed Walrus. "Don't do it!"

"GO!"

VROOM!
Fish pushed a button.

WHOOSH!
The Flycycle lifted itself *straight up into the air.*
"Wow!" screamed everybody.

VROOM!
Fish pushed another button.
WHOOSH!
Bright glider wings locked into place and Fish went flying out across the river.

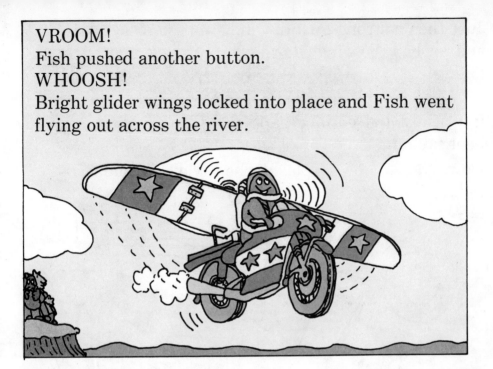

"Ha! Ha!" she called merrily. "Fearless Fish flies again!"

Just then a strong gust of wind swept across the river and pushed the wings down. The Flycycle started falling!

"Uh-oh!" cried Fish. She pushed the wing button frantically, but nothing happened. The Flycycle kept falling.

Down, down, down, splash! The Flycycle disappeared into the river.

Fish came bobbing to the surface. She swam to the riverbank, dragged herself out and collapsed on the ground.

Everyone came rushing over.

"Are you all right?" asked Hippo anxiously. "That was a nasty fall!"

"I think so," said Fish in a weak voice.

"You see, Fish!" cried Walrus. "There *are* lots of things to be afraid of!"

Fish sat up and thought a minute. "Yes," she said. "I'm afraid!"

Everybody breathed a sigh of relief.

Fish took out a pencil and some paper and began drawing. "I'm afraid," she said. "I'm afraid the lock on the wings wasn't strong enough. Now if I just design a stronger lock and maybe use support struts, this can never happen again!"

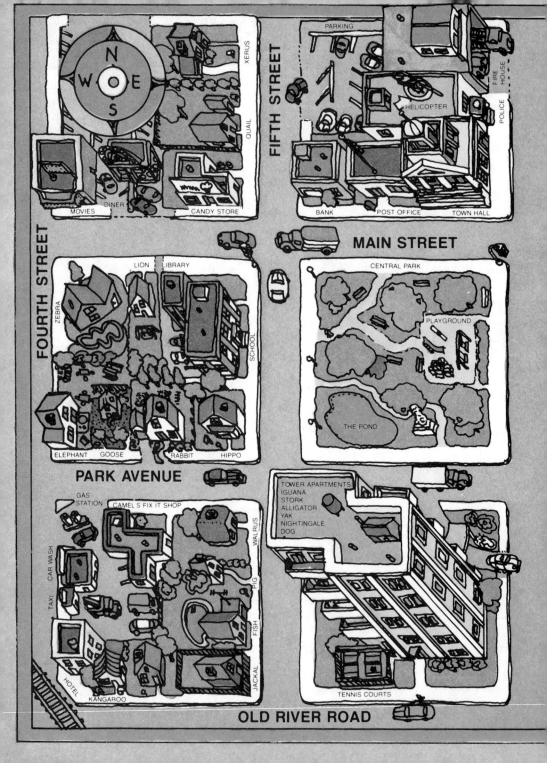